Excitement fills Prime Fire Station. Chief Charlie checks his watch as Cody, Heat-wave and Sparkplug wait anxiously. Chief Charlie looks at the group. "Relax! The new Rescue Bot isn't due for another five minutes!"

3

Suddenly, a thunderous droning noise surrounds Prime Fire Station.

A huge gust of wind sweeps through the station as a helicopter swoops out of the air – and changes into a robot!

"Now *that's* what I call an entrance," Cody introduces himself. "I'm Cody."

The new Rescue Bot grins. "Nice to meet you. They call me Blades."
Heatwave is not impressed. "Showoff," he mutters under his breath.

Just then, the Prime Alert sounds and a voice booms through the Fire Station. "Forest fire! Campers trapped! We have a man on the scene! Rescue Bots respond!"

"You heard 'em!" Chief Charlie orders. "Convert to vehicles and roll out!"
"I'm on it!" Blades takes off. "Not if I get there first!" Heatwave says.

Heatwave quickly converts to fire truck mode.
"Let's go, Cody!" he yells as Cody jumps on board and they race down the road.

Chief Charlie radios to Cody. "Blades' radio isn't working. Our man on the ground is Sawyer Storm – Blades' human partner."
"Got it," answers Cody. "Over and out!"

Heatwave tries to radio Blades from the ground. "Listen, Flybot. *I'm* the leader here and that means that *I'm* in charge."

But Blades doesn't respond, instead racing ahead.
"Wow," Cody says. "He's fast!" Heatwave shifts his gears, picking up speed.

The Rescue Bots arrive quickly, and Heatwave and Cody get right to work battling the fire. Blades hovers overhead.

"Pull up!" Heatwave yells to Blades. "Your blades are fanning the fire and making it worse!" Cody tries to contact Blades by radio. "Blades! Come in, Blades!" But still no response.

Heatwave watches as Blades quickly flies away. "Hmph," he says. "I knew it.
Nothing but a show-off." "Where's he going?" wonders Cody.
"Don't worry about him," Heatwave replies. "Let's take care of this fire!"

Just then, Chief Charlie's voice comes over the radio. "Have you located Sawyer and the trapped campers?" he asks. "Not yet," Cody answers. "The fire's too big and the smoke's too thick!"

Suddenly, Blades swoops down out of the sky, hovering over Heatwave and Cody. "He's back!" Cody yells. "And he's trying to tell us something!"

"I think he's located the campers!" Cody tells Heatwave, who quickly converts to robot mode. "Let's go help Blades and I'll contact Sawyer to let him know we're on our way!" Cody says.

Minutes later, Blades and Heatwave reach the campers. Heatwave battles the blaze, clearing the smoke and putting out the fire. Blades swoops in and rescues the campers. "Got 'em!" Blades yells.

He quickly takes off, bringing them to safety as Cody and Heatwave finish putting out the fire.

Blades and Sawyer arrive back at Prime Fire Station. "Good job, Blades," Optimus Prime says. "I see you've met your human partner, Sawyer Storm."

Sawyer explains, "I was on my way here when I got the call. So I ran to the forest and found the campers. Their campfire was out of control and spreading fast! So I stayed with them until the Rescue Bots arrived."

Just then, Heatwave and Cody arrive back at Prime, covered in soot.
"What took you so long, Hotshot?" Blades teases.
Heatwave laughs. "The name's Heatwave. Great job out there today."

"You *all* did a great job out there," Chief Charlie says. "You worked together and got the job done. I'm proud of you. Now go get Blades' radio fixed!"

As the Rescue Bots head out, Chief Charlie looks at Optimus Prime and smiles.
"They're a fine group of heroes," Optimus says. Chief Charlie agrees.
"I'm looking forward to meeting the rest of them. No more hotshots, I hope."
Optimus just laughs. "You'll see," he answers. "*You'll* see!"